MW01140831

To children of all ages everywhere
and to the loving memory
of Noreen "Pip" Hesthammer, née Jeffery,
Whose warm heart and gentle spirit brought us
the magic of the Stump Gump

Blessings to you from the Stump Gump!

M. Hesthammer

◆ FriesenPress

Suite 300 - 990 Fort St
Victoria, BC, V8V 3K2
Canada

www.friesenpress.com

The original Stump Gump story was written and illustrated
by Noreen P. Hesthammer in the early 1960s.
Before publication in 2021, the story was revised and largely rewritten
by Noreen's daughter, Margit Hesthammar.
Though Margit has made both superficial and substantive changes to
the text, she has done her best to maintain the spirit of the original.

ISBN
978-1-5255-8815-0 (Hardcover)
978-1-5255-8814-3 (Paperback)
978-1-5255-8816-7 (eBook)

1. JUVENILE FICTION, STORIES IN VERSE

Distributed to the trade by The Ingram Book Company

THE
STUMP
GUMP

A little brown stump on the edge of a wood
For many long years had contentedly stood.
Though most of his bark was now holey and crumbling,
He wasted no time on complaining or grumbling.

He made homes for everyone, feathered or furred,
And took care that everyone's songs could be heard.
But toadstools and fungus were growing all round,
And he feared he might shortly sink into the ground...

Now old Mother Nature had planned a surprise—
(Being kindhearted, clever and terribly wise!)
She liked him for thinking not first of himself,
And decided to change the old stump to an elf!

A little brown stump on the edge of a wood
For many long years had contentedly stood.

She told the tall trees to bend over slightly,
So sunlight could shine on the little stump brightly.
She told the fresh rain to sprinkle him well,
And asked a kind fairy to cast a good spell.

The trees and the rain and the fairy obeyed,
And that day the very first Stump Gump was made!
With long legs and arms and leafy green hair,
One minute he wasn't—the next he was there!

The birds and the squirrels kept rubbing their eyes,
As they watched him stand up and look round in surprise.
"Who is he?" they wondered, "and what is his name?"
"I'm Stump Gump!" he cried, "and I'm friendly and tame!"

They danced all around him in happy delight,
And frolicked and feasted till late in the night.
Then they put him to bed in an old hollow stump,
Where he slept like a log—and dreamed like a Gump!

———•———

With long legs and arms and leafy green hair,
One minute he wasn't – the next he was there!

In the morning the Bluebird was first on the spot,
To show the young Stump Gump what was and was not.
How not to fall over when climbing a tree,
And when to be friendly — or not — with a bee.

He must learn all the names of wild creatures by heart,
And Bluebird thought 'Bluebird' was good for a start!
He showed him the best spots to swim in the creek,
And the tastiest twiglets and toadstools to seek.

He must learn all the names of wild creatures by heart,
And Bluebird thought 'Bluebird' was good for a start!

There was so much to see and so much to do,
The days were too short and the hours too few.
He used every second, each wonderful minute,
Till he knew the whole forest and everything in it!

He made friends with Mister and Missus Grey Mouse,
And cared for their babes while they mended their house.
When Elderly Squirrel fell down and got cuts,
He bandaged him up and helped gather his nuts.

But once, after hugging Brown Bear, who was weeping,
He stepped on the tail of Striped Skunk, who was sleeping!
It was quite by mistake, but poor Skunk couldn't tell,
And he scared the young Gump with a terrible smell!

But once, after hugging Brown Bear, who was weeping,
He stepped on the tail of Striped Skunk, who was sleeping!

The Stump Gump raced off to the river nearby,
Where he scrubbed hard, but still came out smelling quite high.
The squirrels and rabbits, the birds and the bear,
All watched from the riverbank, sniffing the air.

Then Bumblebee Family sang, "Here's what to do—
"We'll soak him in flowers!" and away they all flew.
They gathered up pansies and pinks and wild roses,
And every sweet blossom to gladden their noses.

The squirrels and rabbits, the birds and the bear,
All watched from the riverbank, sniffing the air.

They scooped out a hole in the sand by the shore,
  And buried the Stump Gump in flowers galore.
Then they scrubbed him with blooms from his head to his feet,
And when they were done, he smelled perfectly sweet!

The Skunk and the Stump Gump both said they were sorry,
And kindly explained their own sides of the story.
Then all was forgiven and all were delighted,
And merrily cheered for a wrong that was righted!

———••———

They scooped out a hole in the sand by the shore,
And buried the Stump Gump in flowers galore.

When Stump Gump first saw Mister Snake sliding by,
He was startled, and felt a bit nervous and shy.
Mister Snake was quite different from most of his friends —
He moved awfully quickly at both of his ends.

When Stump Gump first saw Mister Snake sliding by,
He was startled, and felt a bit nervous and shy.

But soon Gump could see Snake was playful and kind,
And their differences all disappeared from his mind.
They swam in the river and played on the shore,
Rode down on the rapids and raced back for more!

Then they lay on the beach and looked up at the sky,
Singing songs to the clouds and the birds passing by.
At the end of the day, when they said their good-byes,
They parted with twinkly smiles in their eyes.

———•—

They swam in the river and played on the shore,
Rode down on the rapids and raced back for more!

One day in the midst of a sunny July,
The Stump Gump was counting his friends passing by.
"Five rabbits, two bears and eight skunks I can see,
But it's funny I've never seen someone like me."

"Today," he decided, "I'll look for a Gump.
Perhaps I'll find one in another old stump."
So into the forest he happily scrambled,
Diving through bushes and getting quite brambled.

He poked into dozens of stumps and old trees,
But found no one there—just the birds and the bees.
Then he felt a bit sad and went down to the river,
To cool off his scratches and pull out a sliver.

By the time he was finished, the sky had turned red,
So he gave up his search and looked round for a bed.
He found a good spot in an old hollow tree,
And curled up inside with his chin to his knee.

He found a good spot in an old hollow tree,
And curled up inside with his chin to his knee.

He slept through the night and woke up with a jump,
When Bluebird sang, "Wake up, you lazy old Gump!
There are twigs at the top of this tree that are sweet,
If you wait here, I'll bring you a nice breakfast treat."

Away Bluebird flew to accomplish his task,
And when he came back, the Gump said, "May I ask,
If ever you've seen another Stump Gump,
Green-haired and long-legged and not very plump?"

The bird shook his little blue head and said, "No,
Not here in the forest, but why don't you go
To the pond on the hill by the red cedar stump—
Where I think you'll find someone who's just *like* a Gump."

"...There are twigs at the top of this tree that are sweet,
If you wait here I'll bring you a nice breakfast treat."

By the stump, just a small shiny pond could he see.
"I don't see a Stump Gump," he sighed, "just like me..."
But wait—as he drank from the water so cool,
He *did* see a Gump in the clear crystal pool!

When he smiled, they both smiled; when he jumped, they both jumped.
When he bent over low, their heads almost bumped.
When he ruffled the water, the other Gump quivered,
And when the wind blew, both little Gumps shivered!

It was just his reflection, but still it was fun,
To catch it and lose it and splash in the sun.
Then Bluebird arrived and sat down on his head.
"There, Stump Gump, you've found him—it's just like I said!"

But wait – as he drank from the water so cool,
He did see a Gump in the clear crystal pool!

"Well, it is and it isn't," thought Gump to himself.
"I can't go for walks with this watery elf."
But then, something strange took the Gump by surprise:
A vision appeared in the water elf's eyes!

Stump Gump's throat got a lump and his heart opened wide,
For he suddenly saw who he was deep inside.
Like magic, all creatures—from earthworm to tree—
Had joined up together to make a big "Me!"

He saw how the same water ran through them all,
How the same air made everyone's chest rise and fall.
He noticed that nothing lived all by itself—
Not even a leafy-haired long-legged elf!

He saw how the same water ran through them all,
How the same air made everyone's chest rise and fall.

Since that special day, when the Stump Gump feels sad,
He goes to the pond and comes home feeling glad.
For even though everyone has their own name,
He knows on the inside they're mostly the same!

Since that special day, when the Stump Gump feels sad,
He goes to the pond and comes home feeling glad.

THE END